Racing Through Time on a Flying Machine

Story by Elizabeth Werley-Prieto
Illustrations by Mike Lester

RSVP
RAINTREE
STECK-VAUGHN
P U B L I S H E R S
A Steck-Vaughn Company

Austin, Texas

www.steck-vaughn.com

Library of Congress Cataloging-in-Publication Data
Werley-Prieto, Elizabeth, 1986–
    Racing through time on a flying machine / story by Elizabeth Werley-Prieto; illustrations by Mike Lester.
      p.   cm.
    Summary: Keene finds a time machine and uses it to go back to 1884, meet Thomas Edison, and see some of his inventions.
    ISBN 0–7398–0054–X
    [1. Time travel — Fiction.   2. Edison, Thomas A. (Thomas Alva), 1847–1931 — Fiction.
3. Inventors — Fiction.   4. Stories in rhyme.]   I. Lester, Mike, ill.   II. Title.
PZ8.3.W4655Rac   1999
[Fic]—dc21
                                                  98–37709
                                             CIP   AC

1 2 3 4 5 6 7 8 9 0   03 02 01 00 99 98

To my family, friends, and teachers for all the kindness, inspiration, happiness, knowledge, and words of wisdom they have given me. — **E.W-P.**

For Jessica, Clayton, Anderson, Cameron, Harley, Jack, and Mary Morgan. — **M.L.**

Once there was a boy named Keene,
Who one day found a time machine.
It looked like a clock attached to a seat,
With a place for your head and a place for your feet,
A whole lot of buttons all in a row,
And a little green one that just said GO.
He sat down and wondered just what it would do
If he pushed a button—he wished that he knew.
So he pushed a button that clearly read,
"Visit the Time of Thomas Ed."

5

All of a sudden there was a whir
That sounded like a kitty's purr.
And the whole darn thing began to shake,
Just like a slithering baby snake.
It went up and it went down,
Everywhere and all around.
Then it stopped and a loud voice said,
"We're at the time of Thomas Ed."

The time machine came to a stop,
And then Keene heard a faint clip-clop.
A horse and carriage came riding by,
Topped by a man who looked like a spy.
He wore a long and dark brown coat,
And a deep black scarf around his throat.
Keene turned his head to look around,
And many more interesting things were found:
A mounted cop with his head held high,
And a thin line of smoke trailing up to the sky.
A plaque on each house was engraved with two names,
One for the men and one for the dames.

Keene then parked in a lonely alley,
Where a cluster of rats were having a rally.
Keene walked up every single street,
In search of something good to eat.
On one little plaque the engraving read,
"Mr. and Mrs. Thomas Ed."
"I'll try in here," decided Keene,
"Even though no one can be seen."
He knocked on the door with two brass handles,
And a man came out wearing p.j.'s and sandals.

"Please go away," the man said real quick,
"Because my wife is very sick."
The year Keene knocked upon his door
Was eighteen hundred eighty-four.
That was the year Tom's wife would die
And leave her family all to cry.
But Keene complained, "I've had no lunch.
Could I please have just one thing to munch?"

14

So the man invited Keene inside,
And Keene looked up, and side to side,
A dimly lighted, good-sized house,
In which there lived a good-sized mouse.
But the strangest thing of all to Keene
Was the lights weren't gas or kerosene.
Modern light bulbs lit the room
With a pinkish glow like a flower's bloom.
A bit of music drifted in,
Sounding scratchy like scaly skin.
Tom gave Keene some bread and cheese.
Keene ate it all, and then he sneezed.

AH-CHOO!!!

Tom walked to a table and then sat down,
And turned up the music (Keene hated the sound).
The music machine that sat on the table
Was a phonograph that bore a label.
On the label the printing read,
"Patent Pending, Thomas Ed."
Keene looked at his watch, but it had stopped.
All three hands just flipped and flopped.

16

"It's time that I must leave," he thought,
"Or my mother will be distraught."
 He sadly said, "Good-by!" to Tom.
"I'm heading home to see my mom."

So Keene set out for that lonely alley;
He did not play or dilly-dally.
He found his time machine still there
Where he had left it with utmost care.
He leaped on board, he donned his cap,
And pulled his seat belt across his lap.
He looked at the buttons all in a row,
Including the green one that just said GO.
Keene realized what a thing he had found.
He could travel through time much faster than sound!

He thought, "I could have just a little more fun,
And get back home by the setting of the sun."
Keene went up to outer space,
At the starting time of the lunar race.
He visited Leonardo, too,
And saw some experiments he could do.
But the time got late and soon he knew
He had to go home, so away he flew.

Keene came to the time of his mom and his pop
And pushed the button labeled STOP.
For his whole trip he'd had such fun,
And now this exciting day was done.
But all at once, Keene suddenly knew,
He wanted to be an inventor, too!

Elizabeth Werley-Prieto, author of **Racing Through Time on a Flying Machine**, was in fifth grade at Breakwater School when she wrote her winning manuscript. In 1996, as a third grader, she entered a mystery story in the Publish-a-Book® Contest. It didn't win, so she tried again, this time with great success. Her third-grade teacher, Ms. Clare Ruthenburg, was her sponsor on both occasions.

Rhonda Farnham

Elizabeth lives in Portland, Maine, with her mother, Patricia Prieto, and father, Tom Werley, who are both librarians. She loves writing, art, French, and her four pets (two guinea pigs, a mouse, and a dog named Dudley). Elizabeth has been taking violin lessons for more than six years and plays with the Brunswick Regional Youth Orchestra. She also enjoys modern dance.

Elizabeth has always been interested in writing as a hobby and possible career, and views winning the Publish-a-Book® Contest as a big step toward achieving her goal.

Mike Lester is the author and illustrator of many of his own books. He lives with his lovely wife, Cindy, and their beautiful children, Grady and Hope, in downtown Rome, Georgia.

The twenty honorable-mention winners in the **1998 Raintree/Steck-Vaughn Publish-a-Book® Contest** were Tiffany Chang, Waiakea Elementary School, Hilo, Hawaii; Beverly Nwanna, St. Bartholomew School, Scotch Plains, New Jersey; Jake Horn, Harmony Elementary School, Overland Park, Kansas; Elyse Bledsoe, Green Valley Elementary School, Boone, North Carolina; Joshua Ates, Summerwood Christian Academy, Houston, Texas; Ashley LaPan, Patrick Henry Elementary School, Heidelberg, Germany; Mark Pinske, Trinidad School, Trinidad, California; Meridith Sine, D.L. Beckwith Middle School, Rehoborn, Massachusetts; Rachel Schmillen, Fieldcrest West Middle School, Toluca, Illinois; Ashley Theuring, Ayer Elementary School, Cincinnati, Ohio; Peter Prentiss, Naalehu Elementary School, Naalehu, Hawaii; Kiley Green, La Costa Library, Carlsbad, California; Christy Hough, Sharon Elementary School, Newburgh, Indiana; Frederick Wellborn, Brevard Elementary School, Brevard, North Carolina; Andy Cary, St. Barnabas Episcopal School, DeLand, Florida; Steven Hammes, Waiakea Elementary School, Hilo, Hawaii; Andrea Packer, Salem Christian Academy, Clayton, Ohio; Mark Fox-Powell, The Walden School, Pasadena, California; Bronwen DeSena, Helen Morgan School, Sparta, New Jersey; Michele Lewkowitz, Bayview Elementary School, Fort Lauderdale, Florida.